ENOR

ISBN 978-1-63814-298-0 (Paperback)
ISBN 978-1-63814-299-7 (Hardcover)
ISBN 978-1-63814-300-0 (Digital)

Covenant Books, Inc.
11661 Hwy 707
Murrells Inlet, SC 29576
www.covenantbooks.com

ENOR

Written and illustrated by

C.C. Carson

Once upon a time, on a warm, sunny day, a baby turtle hatched from his egg. This was no ordinary turtle!

This little turtle burst from his egg, ready to see whatever he could see. He was called Enor by his turtle family because of his *enormous* energy!

No one had ever seen a turtle who moved like Enor! He traveled over the riverbank at a gallop, not a slow-moving crawl.

As his brothers and sisters came out of the nest, Enor was rushing from the river's edge and back to the nest, over and over again.

Enor could not understand why the other baby turtles moved so slowly. They could not understand why Enor was going so fast! "Come on, come on!" shouted Enor. "Let's get going!"

As the days and weeks passed, the baby turtles grew and stayed close together. Each little turtle had a special character of its own.

Enor was a burst of energy, like lightning in the sky!

Itsy was a delicate little turtle and loved to sit and watch the dragonflies. She dreamed of being as beautiful and as graceful as those dragonflies, and Enor told her that she was beautiful too.

Flub was fat and lazy, liking nothing more than a nap in the sun on a nice log. Enor especially loved to nudge Flub off the log as he slept and laughed as Flub hit the water with a sound like his name.

Two other little turtle sisters, MeShell and Shelly, were usually together. They loved to stay by a quiet pool of water and see their reflection there. On some days, when the water was clear, it was like looking in a mirror.

Sometimes, MeShell and Shelly argued about who had the most beautiful shell. Enor caught them napping and painted beautiful colors on each of their shells.

How surprised they were when they looked in the reflection pool! Enor laughed as he watched them oooh and aaah at their new beauty.

Enor noticed a bashful little turtle who pulled inside her shell as Enor galloped past her each day on his morning run.

Enor called her SheShy, and soon he became friends with her. SheShy would climb on Enor's back for a ride as he galloped along. She was never afraid when Enor was near. Enor wasn't afraid of anything!

Enor's lack of fear took him far away from his turtle family. For several days and nights, the rain had fallen, and even the turtles had stayed inside their homes.

After the rains stopped, the river grew bigger and roared with all the extra water flowing into it. Enor was excited by the new energy of the river. He went closer and closer.

The river's energy and Enor's energy seemed alike. Enor joined the river and rode the raindrops far, far away. His turtle family was sad and missed Enor, but they knew he was off on a new adventure somewhere.

About the Author

C. C. Carson is a writer of children's books. She lives in a small community in rural Missouri and enjoys her peaceful surroundings.

She is the mother of two children and grandmother of six darlings. She loves to travel and sometimes takes her children and grandchildren with her on an adventure. The shared memories of the family members from these adventures are important to her.

CC is always happy to return to her tranquil rural life, in which her imagination and creative side flourish and fuel her desire to write and illustrate books.

CPSIA information can be obtained
at www.ICGtesting.com
Printed in the USA
JSHW010001310321
13085JS00001B/2

9 781638 142980